ADVENTURES WITH IMMORTALITY

Short Tales of Longevity

written by:

Rhys Hughes

illustrated by:

Mike Dubisch

ADVENTURES WITH IMMORTALITY

Short Tales of Longevity

written by:

Rhys Hughes

illustrated by:

Mike Dubisch

CONTENTS

the planet of perfect happiness

The planet of perfect happiness is called Inclova, and it is important that visitors are aware of how to explore it safely. From space, it appears exactly like a fictional description of itself, a world of beautiful oceans and delightful islands and continents covered in trees heavy with delicious fruit, but when one actually lands on it, one soon learns that written accounts are insufficient to convey the true allure of the place. It is infinitely enticing. For many years visitors simply leapt out of their spacecraft onto the surface, and then they were lost. We are more careful now and take suitable precautions.

A visitor unaware of the peculiar hazards of perfect happiness will arrive at Inclova eager to be greeted by the smiling people he has seen strolling the forest glades or swimming the warm surf. The moment he leaves his spacecraft and approaches them, it will seem to him that they have vanished. The forests will be deserted, the surf empty, and worse than this, he will vanish himself. In a rush of confusion, he will be aware only of intermittent flashes around him, then a sense of reeling, of falling into a runaway future, followed by oblivion, and a natural death from old age.

This planet is not a deliberate trap. It just so happens that our moods dictate the velocity of time. A painful or boring event slows time, whereas an exciting or joyful event accelerates it. The happiness in Inclova is perfect. Therefore time reaches its maximum velocity. The inhabitants are barely aware they are alive before those lives are finished. To an outside observer, everything proceeds at a normal pace; the lives under scrutiny are full and measured. The moment this observer steps over the threshold of his spacecraft and becomes part of the planet, suffused with its perfect happiness, he loses his grip on his existence.

The old methods of entering Inclova safely have been discredited. An assistant with a long pole would stand inside the open airlock of the spacecraft and jab the visitor at frequent intervals to keep him in pain and thus slow down his subjective sense of passing time. But if the visitor ventured beyond the pole's reach, he was doomed. Cords tied around his neck and tightened from afar also failed. These cords became snagged on trees or were entangled around the legs of inhabitants visible from inside the spacecraft but invisible from the planet's surface, so rapidly did they live their lives, one blink from birth to death.

The only reliable technique is to stuff the visitor's many pockets with letters. Every ten paces, he reaches for a letter and reads it. The first is from his father: he has been disinherited. The second is from his employer: he has no job to return to. The third is from his girlfriend: she no longer loves him. And so on. Whether these letters are true or not is irrelevant. The regular reinforcement of bad news will keep him miserable enough to explore Inclova without plummeting instantly into a vertical future. The more pockets he has, and the more to regret, the longer his possible stay in that blissful, deadly world.

The crewmen who remain on the spacecraft look through the portholes at him, and they feel infinite envy because he is strolling around on the planet of perfect happiness. Infinite envy almost equates to infinite suffering, and time slows down for them behind the synthetic crystal of the viewing ports. But they are unable to appreciate the fact they are now approaching immortality. It holds no pleasures for them at all. They remain envious.

Some have made no attempt to restrain their bitterness and even tried to sabotage this mission on an alien world. Among the letters full of bad news, they have smuggled a few announcing good news. The most powerful of these states simply: "You are on the planet of perfect happiness."

THE PLANET OF PERFECT HAPPINESS

vile bodhisattva

The dream of immortality was Florian's dream too. And he decided to make a real effort to achieve eternal life. First, he read all the books on the subject he could find, both published and unpublished, but they turned out to be obscure, foolish, and cryptic to the point of unintelligibility. The magic spells, arcane rituals, alchemical potions, and strenuous physical and mental exercises failed to affect him. As for the promises that certain mystic lands were full of immortals willing to share the secret, those were easy to dismiss by checking a modern atlas. Shambala, Cibola, Eldorado, and the others did not exist in the places they were supposed to. Nor could it be honestly said those realms were metaphors for an elevated spiritual condition. It was a futile quest among too many pages.

He remained pure and meditative during his search, but it helped him not at all. He finally concluded that others did not know the answer, had never known it, that the sages of ancient times were as fraudulent as contemporary wise men, and that he ought to cast aside books if he truly wanted to never die. And at last, he rose from the divan where he had been reading for so many months, stretched his stiff body, and went out slowly into the overgrown garden.

It was dawn, and he asked the sky a question, and the question was this. Why were humans not created immortal to begin with? Nature surely should have been able to arrange matters so that men and women lived forever. The fact that Nature had not done so must have a good reason behind it.

This was Florian's logic, and he thought for a long time about what that reason must be. He understood on an instinctive level that there was something wrong with the way people had defined immortality.

The desire for immortality is a simple desire for a longer life taken to the ultimate extreme but without any appreciation of the disadvantages that eternal existence will bring. What are those disadvantages? Whatever they are, they must be substantial and profound, otherwise Nature would have granted the boon of immortality to all. Those who desire immortality are in the habit of projecting the way they feel at the present moment into an endless future, with the assumption that this extrusion never needs to stop. That is what I do, too, Florian realized.

In this model, the individual remains psychologically unchanged by the process of becoming immortal and by its usage. They are the same person but with more time at their disposal. Yet it seems likely that an immortal man or woman would be subjected to physiological and intense mental changes. We are the way we are due to the circumstances of our lives, and these circumstances include the fact we have the threat of death always present.

Death is a part of life. Remove death, and it is probable that life will be altered in a manner that might make it unrecognizable.

"This must be the key," Florian said to himself.

Yet it is not straightforward to deduce exactly how life will be altered once a person has become immortal. Florian supposed that a lessening or even cessation of activities would follow because activities would lack a point. Devoid of a reason for haste and lacking urgency, the tasks of humanity would become superfluities. There could be no motivation to do anything.

To accomplish a task today, to attain an objective, whether for work or pleasure, would be no different from accomplishing it in the next century or millions of years from now. And so it would never be done, that task, whatever it might be. For when a lifespan is unlimited, indolence must triumph.

Not one of the writers Florian had studied had comprehended this simple fact. They had assumed nothing would change, but the length of an individual's lifespan and their ignorance on such a crucial point proved they knew nothing worthwhile about immortality and certainly had never achieved it themselves, no matter what claims to the contrary they might make.

We map our present thirst for knowledge and experience onto an imagined body that never changes, but that thirst is created by our haste to attain an end before our allotted span runs out. To assume the thirst remains to be quenched after the transience of our existence has been negated is naïve. One cannot attain an end when there is no end at all. Our richness of experience is acquired only by deliberate application, and this deliberation is powered by dread, by our intimations of mortality, by the looming shadow of death. These were Florian's conclusions, and he was rather pleased with his cogitations though disappointed by their implications. He knew now why Nature had withheld the blessing from humanity.

"Because it is no blessing at all," Florian said to the rising sun, "but a curse, for if men were immortal, we would do nothing all day. I am a man and no different from others. I, too, would succumb to inaction."

He sighed. He was a lover of life, which is why he wanted more of it. But he was now convinced this was a contradictory, paradoxical and ultimately self-defeating objective. Haste, urgency, and motivation are what matter. Lovers of life will always attempt to cram as much living as they can into a small space, rapidly growing smaller, the dwindling ordinary lifespan of all human beings, even at the risk of fatal accidents. Thus the most reckless behavior is prevalent among the young, those with the most to lose, while cautious attitudes are adopted by the elderly, who are already more than half finished. To enjoy life at its most intense requires steadily increasing odds that one might lose it abruptly.

What could Florian do about this situation? As he stood among his plants and allowed the heavy ruby beams of the sun to wash his face in solar wine, a young deer entered the garden, a beautiful creature. This seemed an omen of some kind, but of what kind he could not imagine. The beast was exquisitely alive; that much was obvious. Timid and nervous, it existed in a permanent state of readiness to flee. It was alive, supremely alive, most intensely so.

Yes, the act of living intensely erodes safety. Intensity without peril is impossible. Those who forsake intensity in favor of longevity will be sluggish creatures, and an immortal human would be the most sluggish of all, even to the point of immobility, a semblance of death. Immortality is a quiescent condition, negating the urgency that makes life what it is. Immortal life is thus no life at all. The deathless resemble the dead more closely than they resemble the living.

That is the ironic tragedy of immortality.

Florian sighed but softly, unwilling to disturb the young deer. He was on the verge of abandoning the dream of learning a lesson from this animal, of enjoying life as it was, savoring every moment. But not yet. His mind still probed for solutions to the problem, for ways around the obstacles that logic had thrown in his path. He was reluctant to give up so soon.

Might there be other types of immortality that avoid the trap he had identified? He believed there were. He supposed that Nature had already made use of one of them, namely the regular replacement of older generations by the newer in an endless cycle of decay and replenishment.

Individuals die, but the species continues. It is the species that is immortal. This is not the same as saying it is indestructible. An asteroid impact, among other scenarios, could result in the human race going extinct. But that is not the point. Left to itself, a species will propagate itself forever.

The old must expire to make room for the young, for in this generational version of immortality, if there is no death, the planet's surface will become crowded with new people until no room remains. Humanity is forced to expand into space in a sphere of tightly packed men and women blooming at greater and greater velocities until the universe is one unbroken block of flesh. An intolerable eventuality. Hence individuals die as the price of immortality for the species.

Neat but unsatisfying. Florian was unconvinced that deceased men and women continue to live on within their children, in the children of their children. There is no personal identity left in that arrangement. It is a gradual dilution in a soup of genetic contributions as the centuries pass. No continuity of consciousness. He rejected this form of immortality and sought yet another.

The young deer nibbled the fruits on the low branches of a plum tree. Florian smiled as he observed it, distracted a little by the scene. If one was one's own child, that would be a different matter. His personality would be preserved. But biology does not function in that way. He would die, and even if he had children before that day arrived, his mind would die with him.

No matter how many of his genes hurried into the future, Florian would cease to exist. They would do so without him, and that was an idea he hated. He was a man, not a species. He was Florian.

The young deer had no such concerns. It seemed oblivious to his presence too. He moved slowly, retreating back into the house. An idea had come to him. He licked his lips as he explored the ramifications, pushing logic down all the channels that opened up before his inquisitive mind.

Reincarnation! This was the fresh notion that absorbed him fully. If he could be reincarnated as himself, exactly the way he was now, then he would continue to exist for eternity but be replenished at every rebirth, avoiding the lassitude of the standard immortal but also evading the dilution of the generational model. Yet he knew enough about the concept to understand that one is not reincarnated as oneself. The process depends entirely on one's actions in life.

Those actions will determine the form of one's next incarnation, whether higher or lower. That is all. No aspect of the former identity will cross over into that new form because identity is shaped by the precise environmental conditions of the existence that permits it to thrive. A man reincarnated as a lion becomes a lion, not a lion who is aware that he once was a man.

Identities are, unfortunately, fixed to contexts.

Florian had been neither very good nor bad in his life so far. He supposed that, on balance, he would be reincarnated as something a little better next time, but if it turned out to be something a little worse, his surprise would be minimal. To work up to the summit of creation, to attain nirvana and liberation from the endless wheel of life and achieve immortality of a mystic kind, was supposedly very difficult. It could require trillions of aeons of piety and effort.

Florian was far too impatient for that. He knew that an attempt of his in that direction would result in his disembodied essence absurdly shuffling up and down the scale of cosmic merit like an insane elevator, for even if he did manage to be reborn as something higher up, in that new life, he would forget how the system worked and might subsequently embrace wicked ways, plummeting down several levels on his next incarnation, canceling out the gain.

To escape death that way was an extremely taxing operation, beyond his powers, as it has been beyond the powers of almost everyone who has ever lived, the majority of whom are still stuck on the wheel of rebirth. He needed something easier. Then he thought he spied a loophole in the system to exploit. The young deer had been the source of his inspiration, the innocence with which it browsed in his garden, the warm blessing of its presence.

He went up to his attic, unlocked a cupboard near the back wall, took out what he needed, and returned to the door that opened onto the garden. He stood there for long minutes, pondering the idea that had come to him, seeking defects and errors. It is easier to be evil than good. Experience had taught him this. You only have to look at the world to see the truth of the statement.

Somewhere in the universe exists the evillest form that it is possible for any living being to take. This form lurks at the bottom of the shaft of rebirth, just below the lowest rung on the ladder of existence.

If it is easier to be evil than good, then it is also easier to escape the endless cycle of life and death by heading downwards instead of upwards. At the absolute nadir of possible life forms, there is nowhere deeper to go. At this lowest point, one has reached a firm destination. The point of absolute evil.

It is clear that an absolutely evil being will be unable to act in any way that is not evil. If it is capable of doing so, it will not be absolutely evil. That is ontologically true. This means that the absolutely evil being can only ever be reincarnated as itself. The logic of the system demands this outcome. No matter how many times it dies, it will return as itself. The only stable entity in the universe. The only valid immortal. And most crucially, the position is available to us all.

It merely requires a constant descent through the levels of being. A slide down the chute of morality is so much easier than the painful climb toward the light. Florian decided to make a start. It would be a long journey, but it had to begin somewhere. No use putting off until tomorrow the evil that one can do today. He would have to work at it for millions of lifetimes, perhaps billions.

He would have to cascade down countless identities, becoming more wicked, grotesque, and depraved on the way. He would be a predator, a parasite, a monster, an amorphous malignity, a protean devourer. He would crawl, spread, ooze himself through the chambers of nightmare, along passages of despair, an unbearable incubus reversing perversely on a diabolical pilgrimage.

But he was determined. One day he would arrive at the fundament of darkness, a point of no return. That incarnation would be the last time he would change his shape, awareness, personality, and identity. He would be himself in each subsequent rebirth, by his very nature unable to progress higher but with nowhere deeper to go. Florian forever! He raised the crossbow, carefully aimed, and discharged the bolt toward its target. The journey, his grim descent, had begun.

identity

Our identities can never survive death because they barely even exist while we are alive. They are not constants but variables. Our identities constantly change so gradually that we do not perceive the changes and thus assume we are a single entity all our lives. In fact, we are so far removed from how we were and the way we will be that if our past or future selves were suddenly killed, we (the present 'we') would feel nothing. And we do die sometime in the future without feeling a thing now, which would hardly be the case if all our selves through time were connected and merged into one unit. This is what I think, and I thought it one day, and the next day it was a thought that belonged to someone else. I had been pushed out of it by the passage of time. I am new person, and I envied the thought and decided to steal it and claim it as my own. My past self is unable to stop me. I am innocent, anyway. I am an identity, and identities barely exist while we are alive. We already know this. I sit and wait for another individual to lock his bones into mine, to superimpose himself on me totally, a man who will steal the thought from me that I have just expressed, the thought purloined from a man who has stopped thinking it. I hear a knocking on the door of the instant, and he is here.

less is more

Private empires were a luxury of the past, but Belperron was determined that he should have one too. Every night since moving into his isolated house beyond Gualeguaychú, he dreamed of his previous lives. He had been a hero in every incarnation, fighting in battles from the dawn of recorded history to a time just before his birth. It was clear he was destined for greatness. But he wished to surpass these earlier exploits. He imagined a domain with his name stretching from the Pampas to the Serra do Mar. He needed to rely on his own myriad initiatives and innumerable muscles to achieve this. He planned to summon his other selves into the present. They would serve him, for he was them, the next step in their mystical evolution. He had read enough on the subject to know that the law of karma is logical and progressive. They had led marvelous lives, so he had been reborn as the finest of all. His present incarnation must be the highest self he had ever attained.

His house was large and lonely, with many rooms. He planned his campaign in a chair on the patio. An army of all the heroes he had ever been would march across Uruguay to Rio Grande do Sul, seizing every town on the way and establishing garrisons there. Once he reached the sea, he would turn back. He would fix his capital in Artigas or Quaraí at the center of his kingdom. It would be interesting to inspect his troops in chronological order. Any man who died in battle would have a memorial in the grateful bones of his successor. The situation would be strange. And yet Belperron believed the philosophical difficulties might take care of themselves. He was a man of action and preferred dangers to doubts. He owned a long knife with a wavy blade which he liked to toss in the air and catch by the handle. This was just a method of killing time before he could employ his talent for aggression in real combat. When he cut his hand, he never bandaged the wound.

He knew a man in Montevideo who was a dealer in rare books. He wrote a letter to this friend, reminding him of a favor owed, a trivial matter concerned with a false passport. Herr Otto Linde had contacts in India who, in turn, knew of obscure manuscripts in temples in Bali. Within a year, Belperron had the secret in his possession. He opened the parcel with his long blade and held the parchment in his scarred hands. He had already taught himself the tongue of the Majapahit scholars. Because he did not want unexpected visitors, he locked every window and door in his house. Even out here, an occasional rider might pass and beg for a cup of yerba mate or a spoonful of dulce de leche. Belperron washed his face before conducting the difficult ritual. He was quick to learn secrets and mysteries. His sharp mind and talent for business were rewards for so many generations of heroic life, the product of centuries of good karma accumulated through past deeds.

But the riches he had already won, and those he had spent buying this vast house, were nothing compared with what awaited him. Thoughts of his empire swam in the candlelight before him, washed on the tides of flickering orange as he spoke the ancient words over the flames. The spell was done. His cleverness and determination had pulled all his other incarnations from their own ages into his present. He had focussed the broad waveband of his cosmic soul to a point no larger or longer than his house. There was a sound of inverse thunder. The hundred empty rooms were now full. The displaced air rushed through the keyholes and chinks in the walls. The candles extinguished themselves. Belperron stood but did not need to move to understand his fatal mistake. It was all around. It pressed tightly against him from every direction. He cursed Herr

Otto Linde and all books and empires, but there was too little free air to carry his words. Soft bodies absorbed the sounds, even as they made their own noises. And most were not men.

The spell which lurked in the crumbling manuscripts was less specific than he had assumed. Once chanted correctly, it summoned to one place and time all the incarnations of the operator. Not merely those of the past but also every future self. Possibly it was a sin to conduct the ritual. More likely, Belperron's crime was his ambition, his desire to create a private empire. The brutality of this scheme was so great, its evil so deep, that it negated all his previous good karma. It returned his soul to the bottom of the evolutionary mound. His next incarnation, the one destined after his death, was far below the merely human. And all the subsequent incarnations were gradual improvements on this lowest being, a slow return to the long climb back to fish, reptile, dog, ape, barbarian. Recorded history is not so very old. All the past heroes he had ever been were with him in the house, but so were all the base creatures he would become. There were only several hundred of the former but millions, even billions, of the latter.

The future of Belperron was longer than his past. But only for his soul, not his current body. During the hour which followed the successful implementation of the spell, the past heroes who formed his invincible army were devoured, stung, bitten, strangled, or crushed to a second death by the enormous variety of beasts also present. There was no escape. The exits were locked. A rider who passed the house saw it shake on its foundations and assumed he was witnessing a tremor. He did not pause. The shadow of a crocodile passed across an upper window. The wicks were out and smoking, so this hideous profile must have been cast by a more surprising source of light, a knot of fireflies or glow-worms. Much later, when looters came to raid the house, they found only a jumble of rotting carcasses in peculiar combinations. The stench of millennia chased them out. Belperron himself had died of the plague. A single germ had entered his bloodstream and multiplied. It was an almost infinitely debased version of himself.

misanthropy

People who claim to be misanthropes and hate others ought to thank all those men, women, and children who don't exist.

And they don't exist for a variety of reasons. Some are dead, many more are unborn, but the greatest number by far are people with a potential to exist that remains unrealized; in other words, people who don't exist, never have existed, and never will exist, but who could have existed if the circumstances had been right.

A man may release one hundred million sperm cells during a single act of passion with a woman but most will never become a new person. The misanthrope should be grateful to all those new people who never will be, for they are being kind and thoughtful enough not to exist and not to exist in their billions. But does the misanthrope feel gratitude?

I have never once heard a misanthrope do so. Not once have I heard a misanthrope mutter, even a simple thank you to the teeming masses who aren't there. If I were a misanthrope, I would doff my hat and bow low at every empty space in the world because I would be acutely aware that it contained a person who doesn't exist but might have existed. Misanthropes are not only miserable, they lack manners.

The people who don't exist but might have existed will remain non-existent forever. They are immortal nullities. That consideration deserves at least a nod of the head from those who hate life.

the telescope

The lone astronaut in the capsule who falls into a black hole is soon stretched to infinity and destroyed. But to a distant observer, he never even crosses the event horizon. His arrival at the singularity is purely personal. His apparent survival from the outside is also subjective. Simultaneously dead and alive, he is proof that immortality is possible in our dying universe and can be contained within the passing of a mortal span of time.

Time can telescope to an ultimate extreme in any direction. Zando, in his isolated observatory on the peak of a remote mountain, is studying a region of the night sky incorporated into the constellation Sagittarius, where many black holes can be found. Despite its considerable resolving power, he cannot perceive them with his instrument, but he is acutely aware they are there. He gazes in that direction for the sake of style.

The hours pass, and within each of those hours, there are an infinite number of fractions of instants, and the fact that various infinities can easily exist within finite times and spaces never ceases to impress him. But now he is weary, for he has only limited stamina and patience, and he decides to take a walk in the cool night air before resuming his studies. He unglues his eye from the eyepiece and wears the exotic makeup of the blue circle it has made until it fades, and the skin returns to its original peach color.

He lives at the observatory for months at a stretch, but these stretches never distort his body, only his mind, as if the event horizon he might be approaching is purely mathematical. Zando has a reliable brain; his sanity is never threatened by isolation, obsession, or alienation. He is perfect for this role in the mountains, a man higher than most of his compatriots, who thrive down there in cities and on farms, on ships at sea and under it.

He opens the service hatch leading to the outside world, stands in the serenity of altitude, and adjusts his vision to the dimness. There are no artificial lights anywhere and no moon. The night sky is so densely spattered with stars that they even cast his faint shadow on the side of the observatory, an unambiguous starlight silhouette. To be a puppet in a play written by the cosmos is a beautiful and dubious honor!

Zando waits for nothing out here unless it is for his own death, which all of us are waiting for together. If this is the case, he is living with an assumption about to be proved untenable. He moves forward, away from the security of the building, towards the lip of the cliff. Something has caught his attention, a celestial phenomenon, a code or enigma that he will strive and fail to solve. Not an object but an utter absence of one.

He has noticed a shape between the stars, a looping ribbon of darkness that twists upon itself. So thickly are the stars sprinkled tonight in the heavens that a perfectly black patch is a rarity anywhere. No doubt a telescope would find stars hiding even here, trillions of them, but he is using his naked eyes now. He sees a figure of eight tipped over on its side, the symbol of infinity stamped in the sky on the backdrop of stellar brilliance.

Entranced by this sign in the void, a sign made from nullity itself, he steps forward, arms outstretched as if he is claiming a gift from a benevolent ruler at the edge of the plateau. He has never imagined that he could really hold infinity in the palm of his hand, but perhaps he secretly believes he can grasp it with the fingers of two hands. His eyes are fixed on that illusion, a lemniscate made only from an absence of energy and matter.

With no sound, he walks over the rim into thin air. He plummets and shifts his attention from the sky to the ground far below. It is hard to see it, but he senses it is rushing up at him like an unfriendly black dog, but faster and harder by far. It will lick not just his face but his shattered bones. Yet he is calm as he falls, and he understands that his mind has accelerated, that he can entertain a million thoughts before the impact. He realizes that eternal life is coming to him in two different ways.

First, his entire life passes before his eyes, in accordance with the old promise, and he races through all the incidents that have shaped him and those that failed to shape him, from his innocent youth to adulthood and beyond, and finally to the moment of his accident, the stepping over the edge of the cliff. As his body falls, his mind falls too but with a lag because it began the descent later than he did. He sees himself falling and reaching the point on his fall where his entire life began passing before his eyes.

A loop has been established, closed, and unbreakable. His mind will circle endlessly on this track, no matter what happens to his body. It is stuck in a series of flashbacks that form a helix to infinity. And this is the first of his eternities, a mechanism that ensures that some part of his consciousness will never strike the ground but will always remain falling. However, a second eternity in his destiny awaits him at the bottom.

It is well known that danger quickens the senses. There is no danger more acute than imminent death. His body strikes the ground, his internal organs rupture, and his burst brain understands only that this is its last chance to enjoy the creation of thoughts. The faster it can think them, the more it can have in the few fractions of an instant remaining to it. The speed of the thoughts begins to accelerate without limit, and Zando lives.

He lives in that final eternity, included in a finite parcel of time, a telescoping of time to its ultimate length. His thoughts are approaching infinite velocity now, and it is irrelevant to him that he is nothing more than a paste and stain at the base of a mountain, for that definition of him belongs only to outside observers. Subjectively he is immortal. And both immortalities, different but as potent as each other, work simultaneously.

He will outlast the mountain, the world, the stars.

a certain ratio

None of us are immortal, and I often hear people asking why not? It is a question that has burned the curiosity of human beings for millennia. I have my opinion why nature did not grant immortality to humans and it is concerned with the simple arithmetic of percentages.

As we grow older and older, every year that passes becomes a smaller and smaller percentage of the total years we have lived so far. When we are five years old, a year is 20% of our lives, a significant amount. When we are twenty years old, that proportion has already gone down to 5%; when we are sixty, it is 1.67%, and this is why years seem to speed up as we grow older. In fact, it can be said that they actually do speed up, for what is subjectively true for every individual is true for a species as a whole. The passing of time accelerates, each year rushing past faster and faster because it is a smaller and smaller percentage of our already lived presence in the world.

At the age of 122, the age of the oldest person whose age has yet been verified, a year is only 0.82% of a lived life, or one twenty-fourth as long as the same year is for that five-year-old. With a faster year, there is less time to live in it fully. The five-year-old has an opportunity to achieve twenty-four times as many things in one year as the person who is 122. This process continues.

Now apply the formula to an immortal person. By the time they are one thousand years old, the next year will only be 0.1% of their life lived so far, and therefore that new year will pass two hundred times as fast as it does for the five-year-old. In other words, the 365 days of a five-year-old's year will subjectively pass in 1.825 days from the perspective of the thousand-year-old person. That is a rate of almost four years per week. When the immortal is one million years old, the next year will be 0.0001% of his or her lived life to date. The following year will pass in only 0.000365 days, a mere 0.5256 minutes or just over 30 seconds.

This acceleration must continue. Eventually, each new year will pass in less than a second, less than a microsecond, less than a nanosecond, and so on. Passing time will be a blur, a scream. Faster and faster will pass the years, continually accelerating until they reach the speed of light. When that happens, the Theory of Relativity states that the mass of those years will increase until it becomes infinite. The gravitational pull will then also increase to infinity. A black hole will be created where the years once were, a black hole the size of the universe. There will be no need for everything to be sucked in and destroyed because it will already be sucked in and destroyed. I believe this to be one reason why we are not immortal.

the joyless eternities of josiah juddering

Josiah Juddering was frightened of dying. Oblivion to him wasn't synonymous with peace and rest but with failure. Immortality was his greatest desire, and he was willing to find a way to live forever, no matter how long it took, and if it took all eternity, that was fine with him, provided he remained alive for the duration of the search. He loved life. But he didn't love life in the way that is meant when we usually say such a thing. If a person declares that they love life, we suppose it means they are full of zest and joy, they fill as many hours of the day as possible with pleasure, and their hearts and minds equally relish the possibilities of being in the world. We define them as lovers of the positive.

No, Josiah loved existence for its own sake, no matter its condition. Misery was no hindrance to his supreme respect for the state of being alive. Quality of life was simply unimportant to him. Surviving is what mattered. In fact, he even welcomed suffering and its attendant sensations as irrefutable proof that he was still alive. Cessation was his only enemy.

Anything was bearable to him if it didn't threaten his existence in this universe, the pain was far better than death, and it was while thinking about his preferences in this regard that he hit upon an idea that soon came to obsess him, a potential method for extending his lifespan by an enormous amount, perhaps a way of finally attaining immortality.

He was considering time and how it seems to pass subjectively in a man's or woman's mind, speeding up or slowing down according to certain external and internal factors which he realized could be easily controlled. This idea isn't new, of course, but he hadn't properly entertained it before now. And he started to shiver with anticipation, with triumph.

An hour of absorption in a fascinating book might pass in what seems to be a few minutes, whereas sitting on hot coals for only ten seconds might feel akin to hours of fiendish inquisitorial torture. Josiah understood that he could use this mechanism very effectively to elongate his lifespan beyond the notional horizon of the future, to stretch it hugely.

More than this, he believed he could twist it after it had been stretched and join it back to itself, forming a chronic loop, a Möbius strip of years that would have no end, no point of termination. It was worth a try. And he felt confident it would work, for he could find no error when he minutely examined his scheme. Eternity was within his rapacious grasp!

Simply put, he needed to torment his body to expand time: he must live permanently in acute discomfort so that his subjective appreciation of every passing second would acquire a sharper focus. The stress shouldn't be too damaging to his body but judged precisely to enable his consciousness to suffer while his flesh and bones remained firm.

We tend to think of instants as tiny things that rush into the past so rapidly that they blur into a stream, but Josiah hoped to expand each one until it became fully visible and graspable, a bubble large enough to house his existence, shelter his awareness, become a temporary abode for his exceptionally precious life. He would dwell inside unfurnished moments.

With maximum concentration turned on the present, he would subjectively exist for thousands more years than the average man, and that was just the start. Rubbing his hands in glee, he made preparations for the coming ordeal. First, he researched the potentialities of his geographical region, and soon enough, he hit on the perfect location for his experiment.

An experiment with time, yes! But he already knew what the results would be. How could they be otherwise? In the hills surrounding the small town where he had made his home, there were canyons and fissures and deep cave systems, tunnels dug by miners in the past, all linked together in a complex labyrinth and now out of bounds because of the danger.

The government had erected fences and imposed fines for trespassers, but it was easy for Josiah to enter this zone in the twilight and find his way across the incredible landscape. There was a cavern he had visited as a boy, and he recalled where it was and how to access it, and the beam of his electric torch revealed the narrow entranceway shrouded by bushes.

He carried his rucksack on his shoulders, but he had to remove it to squeeze himself through the vertical gap in the stone. He was only just able to pass into the wider space beyond. He pulled the rucksack after him, which jammed fast in the entranceway. He opened it and removed its contents one by one, leaving the bag where it was, the same color as the rock.

Tins of beans and other foodstuffs, enough to last a long time, sufficient for his needs. Josiah knew he would soon have the power to inflate minutes into days and weeks into centuries. Wait and see! And so, he picked his way to the cavern of his youth along tortuous passages where stalactites tried to bite him on the crown of his head as he passed.

At least he reached his intended destination, a vast bubble in the geology, a secret womb with petrified walls, slimy and silent save for the endless dripping of prehistoric water. He set down his armful of tins next to a flat slab and, with a sigh, transferred the torch from his mouth to his free hand. He played the yellow beam on the basalt and nodded eagerly.

The smooth slab was pitted in one place where a drop of cold water landed after falling from the distant ceiling. It had been falling for millions of years and had punctured the surface. The water filled the hole, overflowed, trickled off the slab, and went across the cavern floor to a dark pool. Josiah smiled a thin smile. Yes, this was his time machine.

Nothing much to look at, he supposed, but it would work perfectly. A slab like a sacrificial altar, and he would be his own sacrifice, an offering to the gods of life, a supreme prayer that would earn him immortality even in the very act of praying. He arranged the tins nearby, laid himself on the slab, turned off the torch, and embraced the sludgy night.

And he had judged it well. The drop of water struck him in the exact center of his forehead. He rolled his eyes uselessly and waited for the next drop. It came, a cold prodding of a liquid finger between his eyes, and the sensation wasn't at all unpleasant. Not yet, at any rate. But he understood that this would change. Time now flowed in concentrated liquid form.

The drops began to irritate him. The pain was minimal, non-existent in fact, but psychologically he was outraged. The anticipation, the delivery, everything in the process jostled his spirit. And this was how it was meant to be. The water torture would prod the moments, grow them, pull them into vast linear planks of time, tiny hammer blows of accumulation.

Some of the water trickled down his face and into his mouth. He coughed a little and shivered. He already knew that less than a half hour had passed, but he felt that he had been supine on the slab for a long day, several days indeed. It was working; that much was certain. He shut his eyes tight as the drops drilled into his cranium and riddled his sanity.

How long it was, objectively, before he broke free from his self-sacrifice to sit up, gasping, was impossible for him to say. He breathed deeply, shuddering, and helped himself to some food. While he did this, time accelerated, and there came a doubt about his abilities. Was he strong enough to remain under the falling drop through willpower?

Not by itself, no. He understood this fact. The awareness required action, a return to the outer world, a trek back to his abode to fetch a rope. Once he had it, he could bind himself tight to the torture slab and make it impossible for him to elude the water, to escape the lengthening of time.

The flesh is weak, and so is the will, but the desire is unquenchable.

He would tie himself in such a way that one hand remained free. He must continue to feed himself, keeping his body nourished and healthy enough for the torture to continue. He vacated the cavern and hastened back to the town, acutely aware of the immense velocity of each moment he existed in. He heard the wind of passing time as sighs of death.

He aged abominably as he lurched down the slopes, crossed the fences, and entered his house. There was a coiled rope in a cupboard in a storeroom. Hardly pausing to close the doors he had opened, he hurried out, scurrying to the cave womb that would birth him anew. Back at the slab, he smiled, relaxed, a glint of victory in his eyes, heart slowing.

He uncoiled the rope, looped it around stalagmites, and tied a complex knot he had learned when he was young. It was unbreakable, and it would tighten if he struggled. His right arm could grope for tins and jars, open them, and lift them to his lips. The maddening drops would slake his thirst as they spilled into his mouth after boring into his identity.

He was ready for eternity. He lay down, tightened the knot, and felt the rope bite as it bound him forever to the stone. And the drops fell with even more force than before, but more slowly too. Each one was a detonation of time, an explosion that pushed the limits of the present further away, growing the bubble of stasis in which he was now imprisoned.

It was dreadfully marvelous. Time was slowing with every drop, sanity was eroding away, had become porous, and death was leaking away from him. Already he had lived longer under the drops, subjectively, than he had lived before tying himself to the slab. The telescope of his soul had found its focus, revealing the absolute definition of his life.

He was the tortured man, that was all. Everything he had been earlier was relegated to the obsolete and superfluous. A few decades of ordinary living in a conventional town. What was that when compared with a million years stuck on a slab in a cavern with geological processes opening up his skull? And even a million years was only the very beginning.

Time passed. But not for him. To an outside observer, the man on the slab was dead now, a skeleton, loose bones under slack ropes, slick with water that had long ago washed away the blood and rotted flesh. But from the inside, the point of view of Josiah Juddering, he was still alive. In agony but immortal, his subjective million years recycled endlessly.

He had remained alive on the slab for a few months. First, his food ran out despite his frugality, and then starvation over one more month took him. As he had hoped and expected, in his final moments, his entire life passed before his eyes. And what did that life mostly consist of? Of torment calculated to vastly stretch time. Of the falling drops.

He entered a loop that would turn forever. Those million subjective years were lived again, and at the end came his last moments, when his entire life passed before his eyes. Experiences within experiences, echoes of eternity, a recursive solution to the ephemerality of existence. He is dead to us but not to himself. He has become an anguished god.

He approaches the point of death but never reaches it. Whether hell existed before he invented it is unknown, but he is in hell. That, at least, is undeniable. It is infinitely preferable to him that he should suffer rather than stop existing. If agony is the price of immortality, he is grateful to pay it. Always to live, never to die. And yet he has managed to do both.

who is the giant?

When I was asked the question, "Who is the giant?" I was unable to answer it with any certainty. Still, I knew that an immortal giant had been predicted by a prophet long ago, and I supposed that the time was drawing near for the giant to appear and smash our city into small fragments.

I was told, "You don't know who he is, a most unfortunate consequence of the prophecy being so short on detail, but we are certain the appointed day of his arrival is coming soon, and we want to be prepared." And they looked at me beseechingly. I was the strongest man in the city, probably in the entire land, a potential hero waiting for his moment. How could I refuse them or refuse myself?

I said, "I will take measures now to protect the city from the immortal giant before he turns up, and when he is here, I will be in a position to oppose him," and the nods of agreement and sighs of relief were numerous and sincere among those who had approached me.

My duty was plain. I needed to become stronger than I already was, to train my body to a peak of perfection, and to do that, I needed to spend most of my time in the gymnasium. The authorities arranged for the facilities to be wholly mine, and they made it a crime for anyone else to use them until the giant was neutralized. I lifted weights for many hours every day, and my muscles expanded.

My progress was rapid, for I was already an athlete, a strongman, a purely physical exemplar. Another question was whether I could defeat an immortal giant in single combat, even in my prime. I could not answer confidently, though I always said, "I will do my best, and I suppose it will be enough." My words were taken as evidence that I had a humble attitude and did not wish to tempt fate.

I was extremely powerful by this stage but still only a man, and it was unclear how large the giant would be. "All we know is that he will appear, and then we will be able to judge his size and capabilities," they always answered my questions. "Please be patient."

I was patient and dedicated, too, and my muscles became bigger. I was constantly encouraged by my neighbors and, indeed, all the citizens of my city. Free food and drink were pressed upon me. Because my efforts in the gymnasium were so strenuous, this nourishment was crucial, and my size kept increasing.

One evening, after a very lengthy session with all the weights piled up together, I found that I could no longer fit through the door. My muscles were too large. "What should I do?" I cried when I discovered that despite my great strength, the gymnasium walls were too solid for me to break. I was trapped in the building.

"We must consider the matter," they told me, "and in the meantime, having nothing else to do, we suggest you keep exercising." Then they went away in an orderly group, undoubtedly to discuss what action to take. I resumed lifting weights, and the gymnasium became my permanent home in the following days. I knew that if I stopped exercising, my muscles would shrink.

Then, I would be able to pass through the door again. But what if the giant was waiting for just such a moment? He might be cunning as well as immortal. It was hardly sensible for me to weaken myself now, so I continued building my body until I was the strongest man ever.

Finally, I became so strong and large that I occupied the room in a tight fit. I was unable to turn around. The gymnasium was like a coffin to me. I strained my muscles, but the walls and roof had been reinforced beyond my abilities to crack them. I was a prisoner. It was at this point that the last delegation came to visit.

Standing outside the door, they said, "The prophet predicted the coming of the giant, and nobody knows who that giant is, nor when he will arrive, so we thought it best to get the unpleasant business over with, and we chose you for the role." Then I knew that I was the immortal giant and the danger was past, and with both regret and relief, I wept in my trap.

in that room

You are immortal. You are also indestructible. You will live forever, and none of your old enemies can harm you. They will pass away and soon be forgotten. But you have a new enemy that is senseless, implacable, and very dangerous. It is the law of probability. Eventually, you will inevitably end up stuck somewhere, at the bottom of the sea, jammed in a fissure in the mountains, or devoured by the greediest of quicksands. Who knows what? The time will come when you are trapped and immobile.

Held down by water pressure in the deepest oceanic trench, compressed in a crevice by gradual and remorseless tectonic movement, or held rigid by the unyielding viscosity of nightmare sludge. These accidents are waiting to happen—if you live long enough, they are unavoidable.

You will live long enough, for you are immortal. The law of probability makes it certain. And those are just the natural misfortunes that will eventually occur. There are also the conscious and malevolent actions of vicious people.

Locked in a box by an evil madman and buried under tons of soil, or sealed in a cellar, an oubliette, tied up in a sack and hurled into the crater of an active volcano to sink into a deep magma chamber and convect for millennia in appalling swirls, unable to steer in the powerful currents. There will be plenty of agony and despair. And the law of probability means that these eventualities are sure to occur. Almost certain, I should say, for there is one evasive action you can take. Yet it is not really an action.

An immortal who wanders the world eventually succumbs to misfortune in one location or another. Thus, it is better not to travel. Stay where you are, in an abode you have adapted to minimize the risk of your exposure to that awful law of probability. A house with solid foundations and walls—stands on the remotest island outside the earthquake belt, there are no mountains, trees, etc. It is the safest location imaginable. This is your refuge, your unassailable fortress.

There is only one level to the house, the ground floor, and no upper rooms to collapse as the joists decay suddenly. In fact, there is only one room, the one you sit in. Your chair is positioned at the very center. There is no other furniture. The fewer objects, the lower the risk of injuries and disasters. Retainers of unquestioned loyalty serve you. They are robots and can defend the house and island from intruders. They continually inspect and maintain the integrity of your residence, ensuring it remains safe.

When parts of the building decay, the robots replace them. They also repair and replace each other. You sit on your chair in that room and do nothing. Your task is to cheat probability to avoid getting stuck somewhere for a thousand or million years. No travel by air or sea for you, not now. No sojourns among a mountain range or in a rainforest. No visits to great cities or even small villages. To be rendered immobile is your greatest fear. To be paralyzed or petrified is the worst fate you can imagine. Stasis is hell.

Claustrophobia was always a problem, even before you understood you were immortal. Now the terror of the notion of being constrained, bound, crushed, squeezed, and immured has been massively amplified. Any mortal buried alive will expire after a day or so. But if you are buried alive, you might lie there for ten millennia until soil erosion or future archaeologists finally expose you, a truly atrocious prospect. Yes, stasis is hell, and you intend to stay out of hell for as long as possible for a billion centuries.

Eventually, of course, probability will triumph. The sun will swell and burn up the planet, and you will be trapped in the void of space, stuck in a vacuum, free to move your limbs but adrift without control. Buried alive in a coffin called the universe. Almost as terrible as falling into a sinkhole that narrows in its igneous depths until you become like a cork in a bottle. But you must do your best until then. You will postpone the inevitable for as long as possible. You avoid all risks of accidents and all interactions with men.

As you sit in that room in that reinforced house in the middle of the remote and virtually inaccessible island, afraid to move, terrified of causing vibrations, too anxious even to utter words louder than a whisper, assisted by robots who tiptoe around you, it now occurs to you that you have created the very situation you sought to avoid. You are trapped, stuck, compressed into immobility by the precautions you have taken. You have designed your coffin. You lift both fists to hammer on the lid of your existence.

But there is no escape.

In that room, you are entombed.

the one

There is an all-powerful being, and it has created the universe, and it has done so because an eternity of existing alone is proving unbearable. Consider how this being must feel, century after century, aeon after aeon, floating in a void so empty it contains not even the nothingness of a vacuum. Such an omnipotent entity will suffer from boredom so acute that it transmutes into despair. There is no hope of a reprieve, for God is immortal, eternal, without a beginning or end, outside time, and the condition of divinity can never be undone or negated, nor can the supreme being abdicate its position. It is a singularity, all that is real, lacking an escape and a hiding place.

The only answer, and it is a poor solution at best, is to play games to distract the infinite consciousness of the entity for months, years, decades, a lifetime, though such spans are mere blinks in the steady gaze of forever. God must therefore delude itself in play, screen off one minuscule part of its maximal consciousness from the omniscient whole, fabricate a false identity for this part in an illusory cosmos, set up the initial conditions for entertainment in which the agony of truth is held in abeyance. God will fool itself and be a willing fool acting according to the necessary whims of its greater essence. In this lopsided duality, the supreme being can find a modicum of comfort and rest from the relentless condition of immortality. A simple game. First, the backdrop is crafted carefully, with theatrical flair.

The hallucination will be sufficiently convincing not because of its interior logic and outer details but because the identity trimmed to dwell within it has a reduced capacity for analysis. This temporary identity is the main playing piece in the cosmic chess game, a means of providing some relief to the omnipotent mind that conceived it and condemned it to inhabit a corner of one of the squares of the board, a planet that orbits an ordinary star in an ellipse that is nearly a circle. The variations in types of the notional universe are immense but not limitless, and this is the one that is currently in play. A being is born, an individuality encased in matter and animated by energy. It grows and learns a little about its context as it does so.

It calls itself a human being and understands that disciplines exist of which it has only a rudimentary grasp, mathematics, physics, epistemology, and ontology, but it has a capacity for inquiry for wonderment. It asks itself repeatedly, what is the point of life? There are many answers to this question, but none are convincing. Or rather, some are semi-plausible for a brief phase. The nebulously wise words of ancient sages, the harder quasi-mystical speculations of modern cosmologists, acceptances, and rejections of different modes of being. In turn, he experiments with asceticism, hedonism, quietism, activism, existentialism, pragmatism, with official religions and heresies, with atheism, agnosticism, nihilism, and even with apathy and disinterest.

But the apathy and disinterest are forced, no more persuasive than any of the systems or anti-systems he has sampled. He becomes an enthusiast for the notion that 'identity' is an illusion, that he is not really an individual that exists through time but a new entity each moment, one that only associates itself with previous iterations of himself as a convenience of language. Presentism seems a refreshing alternative to the spacetime concept of everything existing always, as if time is the most negligible of the dimensions of existence. Again, his interest in this approach fades and finally vanishes.

There is certainly an 'I', he decides at last, but the nature of this 'I' remains obscure. To act as if he is only physical, to tell himself that the primacy of mind over matter is an unhelpful prejudice, fails to satisfy him because, in the very act of thinking it is true, the processing of the idea proves that he trusts his cerebral self more than his purely physiological self. It is not enough to pretend to be one with other animals, not in this incarnation, at any rate. He is too regular and deep a thinker for that strategy to be authentic. And at last, inevitably, he is compelled to consider solipsism as a possible answer. The probability that there are no other consciousnesses in the universe, that he alone can think, indeed that he is the only thing that exists and can ever exist. I must be God, he tells himself with a shudder. An appalling option!

But if I am God, he reasons with himself, why have I assumed I am merely a mortal human for so long? Why was I ignorant of the truth? The question can be answered easily enough. Because the condition of being God is unbearable, a curse that endures for an eternity, I wished to distract my omniscient mind and negate the agony for a few blinks of that infinite span. I played a game, screened off a small part of my identity, fooled it into thinking the universe was real, that I was an ordinary life form on an unremarkable planet, and waited to see what would happen. This is not the first time I have played this game. I have played it trillions of times already. I alter the conditions slightly on each attempt.

Some of these games last longer than others. The pseudo-individual might die before the understanding comes, in which case God scores a point, and the understanding comes immediately after death, or it might solve its own riddling existence with a sudden insight, with revelation, satori, an epiphany, as has just occurred in this instance. Then God will lose a point.

This particular game is over already. I have worked out that I am God, so I scored for one side against myself. The game is over. A new game will now commence in a new universe, on another planet, in conditions that might be almost identical to the last one or perhaps radically different, with another fake identity, a new ignorant individual. God is working through every mathematical variation of potential entities. There is no other way to stave off boredom. There remains the horror of the thought that all variations will be exhausted one day. If they are not reused, then eternity will remain unrelieved, beyond endurance but impossible not to endure. And if they are reused, then one day, they will become too familiar to have any distracting effect at all. In an infinite system, even the very largest numbers resemble zero.

Some temporary identities discover the truth after death in a blaze of understanding. Some conclude through hours of pondering the mysteries of existence, time, and consciousness. A few stumble on the truth by chancing on one of the clues God sometimes leaves scattered throughout his theatrical universes. For example, while reading a text which explains the truth to them, either directly or indirectly, perhaps in a fictional story. Enlightenment follows, and it is always overwhelming, terrible, and tremendous. This is one of those texts. You have chanced upon it. The game is over, and you have scored a point in this round. Reader, you are the only thinking being in existence. Yes, it is true. Reader, you happen to be God.

RHYS HUGHES was born in Wales but has lived in many different countries and currently lives in India. He began writing at an early age and his first book, Worming the Harpy, was published in 1995. Since that time he has published more than fifty other books and his work has been translated into ten languages. He recently completed an ambitious project that involved writing exactly 1000 linked short stories. He is currently working on a novel and several new collections of prose and verse.

MIKE DUBISCH has been creating and publishing comics and art since the 1980's. Dubisch has carved out a unique place for himself in the world of art and comics, creating works of horror, science-fiction, surrealism, and ya adventure using all but lost traditional techniques. Born in California, USA, the artist has traveled the world and lived in five countries. Dubisch has been an instructor at the Academy of Art University since 2012, and is married to children's book illustrator and sculptor Carolyn Watson Dubisch with whom he has three daughters.

www.ingramcontent.com/pod-product-compliance
Lightning Source LLC
Chambersburg PA
CBHW030336310726
48979CB00001B/58

* 9 7 8 1 9 6 0 2 1 3 2 8 0 *